THE
WILD

For Custard the Duck and Rosy
who lived with us in The Wild

This edition published 1994 by
Diamond Books
77–85 Fulham Palace Road
Hammersmith, London W6 8JB

First published in Australia 1986 by Lothian Publishing Company Ltd
Published in Picture Lions 1989

Picture Lions is an imprint of the Children's Division,
part of HarperCollins*Publishers*

Printed in Great Britain

PICTURE
TEDDY

THE WILD

Bob Graham

Here is Russell's house,
on the top of a hill,
at the edge of a forest.

Here is . . . . The Wild.

Look closer.

Here is Russell
reading late at night,

with a little light
perched over his
book like an insect.

His sister's name is Mary.
She sleeps on the edge
of the bed.

Her toy animals make quite
a crowd. They sleep with
their eyes open.

His mother and father are fast asleep in their bed,
the moon shines softly through the trees, it fills
the room and colours his father's head pale blue.

Look closer still. Rosy coughs and snorts
in her sleep. She is old and friendly
and smells like a bear.

Molly is young and crazy and never still,
even when sleeping. Her front legs twitch
as she dreams of chasing rabbits and sheep.

The Duck sleeps in her own box. It is
warm and lined with straw, but a little cramped.

Russell is reading *Return to the Wild*,
about a lion from the zoo that is taught
to hunt . . . then returned to the plains of Africa.

In the morning, Russell discovers
that his rabbit, Blackberry, has returned
to The Wild, through a hole in the wire.

Then he finds that
his frog, Herman, has also
returned to The Wild,
over the glass wall of
the fish tank.

He is pleased to find
his tortoise is still
sleeping like a rock
in the drawer.

Russell is very worried. How will his pets survive?
"Let's get the dogs. We will track Blackberry and
Herman through The Wild."

But the dogs aren't very good at tracking. The wind is up and Molly is wild. She leaps at old Rosy and bites her on the heels.

"It's the sheep dog in her," says Mum.
Does Molly think Rosy looks like a sheep?

Deep in the forest it is still and quiet. There are places with tangled trees and ferns and the smell of foxes,

places that are silent and cold, and deep dark green

and places that drip.

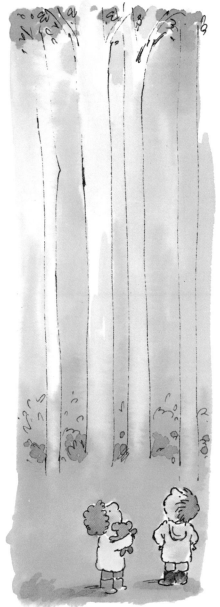

"They're not up there," says
Russell, "Blackberry and
Herman don't climb trees."
"Mary is just looking at
the sky," says his Mum.

"They're more likely to be
down here," says Russell.
But they weren't.

Mary has lost interest in the search;
there are too many other interesting things to look at.

"The way that dog is crashing around, there won't be
a rabbit or frog within miles of here," says Dad.
"No sheep either," says Russell.

Mum throws sticks for Molly who drops them
all wet and slippery at her feet.

The mist is rising with the moon. This is
a better place for Wild animals than families.
The searchers head for their house on the hill.
"I'm sorry about your animals," says Dad.

Look through the window. Rosy settles in her
own special place in front of the fire. She
lies there with steam gently rising from her coat.

Russell's father plays with
Molly for hours. He has
dog hairs all over him.

He pokes his shiny
head at Molly and they
wrestle on the floor.

Molly then sits on
Rosy's head, but
Rosy doesn't stir.

The Duck is not so playful.
Russell's father pushes his
dome in the Duck's direction . . .

. . . and gets three sharp taps. The Duck
waddles away with its wings on its hips.

In the morning, it pokes at unseen things in Rosy's coat . . .

then it goes low and snakey and pecks at
Russell's mother when her back is turned.

The Duck is the boss of the garden.

It flaps its clipped
wings at the fence.

It needs somewhere
to swim.

The Duck needs more space, it needs The Wild,

and *that* starts at the garden fence.

Russell and his family have decided they will
pack the Duck in its box,

and take it to the lake in the park.
It may not be really Wild,

but Russell has heard that foxes raid the rubbish
bins at night, so the park could be a bit Wild.

Russell would like to sail the Duck on a piece
of string like a boat, then bring it back
home. But that would not help at all.

So the Duck returns to The Wild.

The family return to the house on the hill.

Russell returns to his bed and his book, and thinks
of his rabbit and frog returning to The Wild together.

Will they meet up with
the Duck?
Can they find food

or do they have to be taught
to look after themselves like
the lion in his book?

Molly sleeps on Mary's bed. Molly dreams of chasing sheep.

Russell and Mary's mother and father sleep soundly. Their father still has red peck marks on his head.

Rosy steams and smells by the dying fire. She will never leave.

The small light in Russell's room goes out.

In the morning,
Russell can't find his
tortoise *anywhere*.